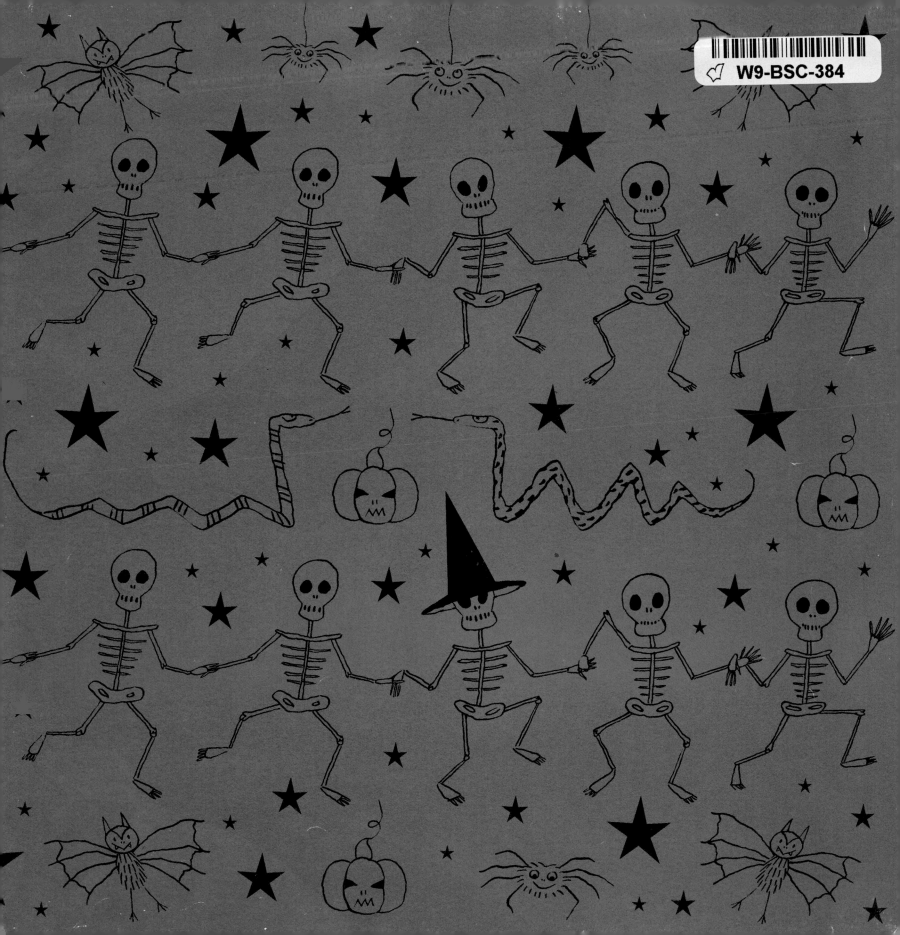

W9-BSC-384

For the good witch in all my girls. —TS

For Dad. —RB

Copyright © 2017 by Teri Sloat
Illustrations copyright © 2017 by Rosalinde Bonnet
Cover art © 2017 by Rosalinde Bonnet
Cover design by Kristina Iulo and Jen Keenan
Cover copyright © 2017 Hachette Book Group, Inc.

All rights reserved. In accordance with the U.S. Copyright Act of 1976, the scanning, uploading, and electronic sharing of any part of this book without the permission of the publisher is unlawful piracy and theft of the author's intellectual property. If you would like to use material from the book (other than for review purposes), prior written permission must be obtained by contacting the publisher at permissions@hbgusa.com. Thank you for your support of the author's rights.

Little, Brown and Company

Hachette Book Group
1290 Avenue of the Americas, New York, NY 10104
Visit us at lb-kids.com

Little, Brown and Company is a division of Hachette Book Group, Inc.
The Little, Brown name and logo are trademarks of Hachette Book Group, Inc.

The publisher is not responsible for websites (or their content) that are not owned by the publisher.

First Edition: July 2017

ISBN 978-0-316-25673-5

10 9 8 7 6 5 4 3 2 1

APS

Printed in China
The illustrations of this book were made with India ink and watercolor on 300 lb Moulin du Roy hot pressed paper and finalized with Photoshop. The text was set in Providence Sans and the display type was hand-lettered by the illustrator. This book was edited by Mary-Kate Gaudet and designed by Kristina Iulo and Jen Keenan with art direction by Saho Fujii. The production was supervised by Erika Schwartz, and the production editor was Annie McDonnell.

Zip! Zoom! ON A BROOM

Teri Sloat

Illustrated by

Rosalinde Bonnet

LB
LITTLE, BROWN AND COMPANY
NEW YORK BOSTON

One goes zip. **Two** go zoom.

Three witches glide from room to room.

Four soar high.

Five dive low.

Six haunt the basement down below.

Seven chant.

Eight incant.

Nine wicked witches rave and rant.

Ten take off, packed too tight.
Ten witches bicker, start to fight.

Ten witches push.

One shouts a curse,

"Broomstick,

zoomstick!

Hit reverse!"

Nine witches squabble, squirm for room.

One
topples
from the
plunging
broom.

Eight witches cast an ancient spell.

One witch goes POOF!

So long! Farewell!

Seven

spiral

through

a cloud.

One
witch
whirls
off,
shrieks
out
loud!

Six plummet down,
still holding on.

One gets zapped
by lightning—
gone!

Five witches drenched; they moan and groan.

One slides off, soaked to the bone.

One grip is slipping.

Four witches dripping in the sky.

Three upside down, still clinging tight.

One somersaults

into the night!

Two witches dropping to the ground.

One jumps off, lands safe and sound.

One witch yells
her spell in time,

"Broomstick, zoomstick! Start to climb!"

One witch glides across the moon.